This Walker book belongs to:

_____

_____

_____

To Marin, Vincent and Max

First published 2009 by Walker Books Ltd, 87 Vauxhall Walk, London SE11 5HJ
This edition published 2011 for Bookstart 10 9 8 7 6 5 4 3 2 1
© 2009 Petr Horáček The right of Petr Horáček to be identified as author/illustrator of this work has been
asserted by him in accordance with the Copyright, Designs and Patents Act 1988
This book has been typeset in Horacek Printed in China All rights reserved No part of this book may be
reproduced, transmitted or stored in an information retrieval system in any form or by any means,
electronic or mechanical, including photocopying, taping and recording, without prior written permission from
the publisher British Library Cataloguing in Publication Data: a catalogue record for this book is available
from the British Library ISBN 978-1-4063-4030-3
www.walker.co.uk

Petr Horáček

HAN T

WALKER BOOKS
AND SUBSIDIARIES
LONDON • BOSTON • SYDNEY • AUCKLAND

I asked Grandad to play football
with me, but he was too busy.

I went to
see Grandma
but she was
busy too.

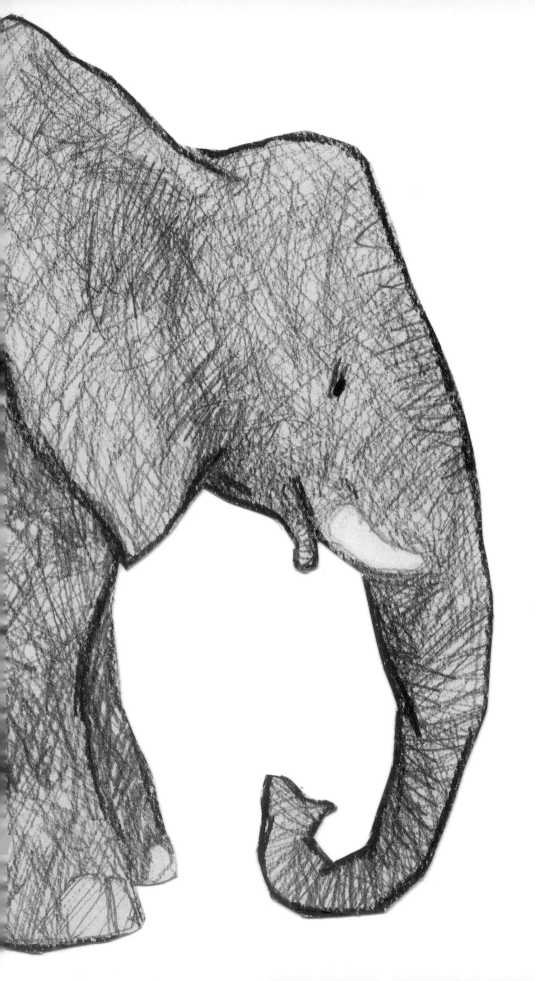

So I
asked my
ELEPHANT
if HE
wanted
to play
with me.

We played football
in the garden.

Then Grandad called,
"Who MESSED UP
the flowerbed?"

"I'm sorry,
it was my
ELEPHANT,"
I replied.

Grandad did not believe me,
so I took my ELEPHANT inside.

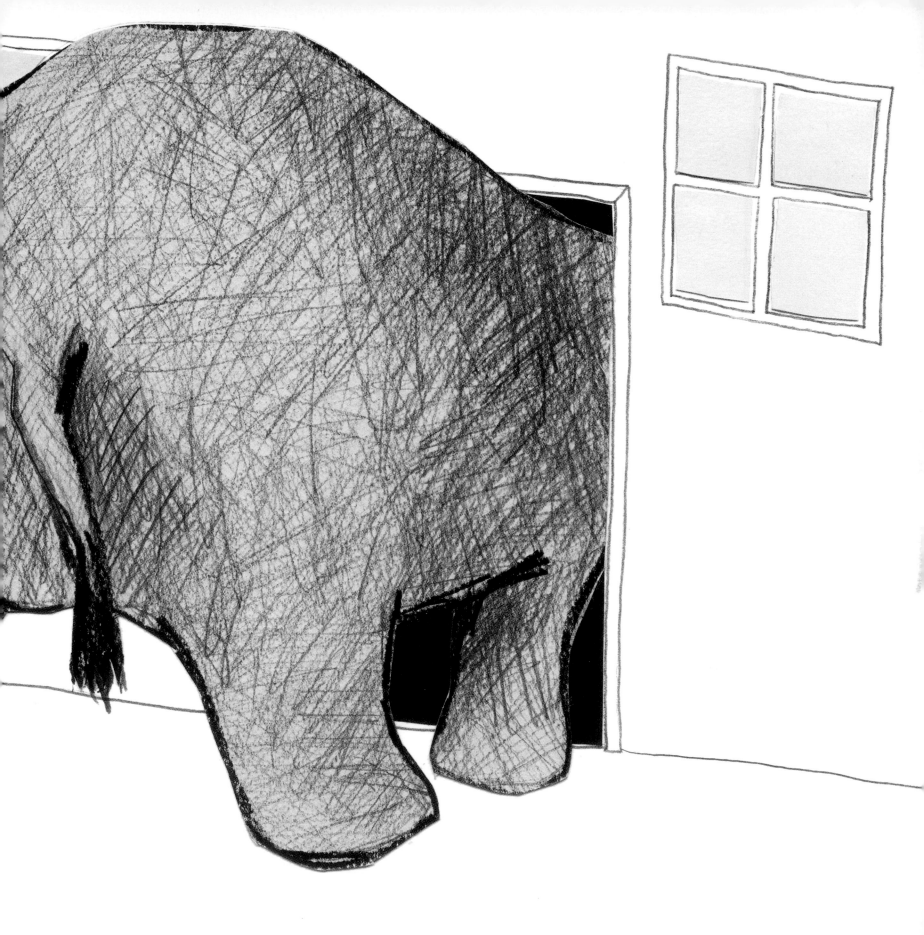

Then Grandma called,
"Who MESSED UP the hallway?"

"I'm sorry, but it must have
been my ELEPHANT,"
I replied.

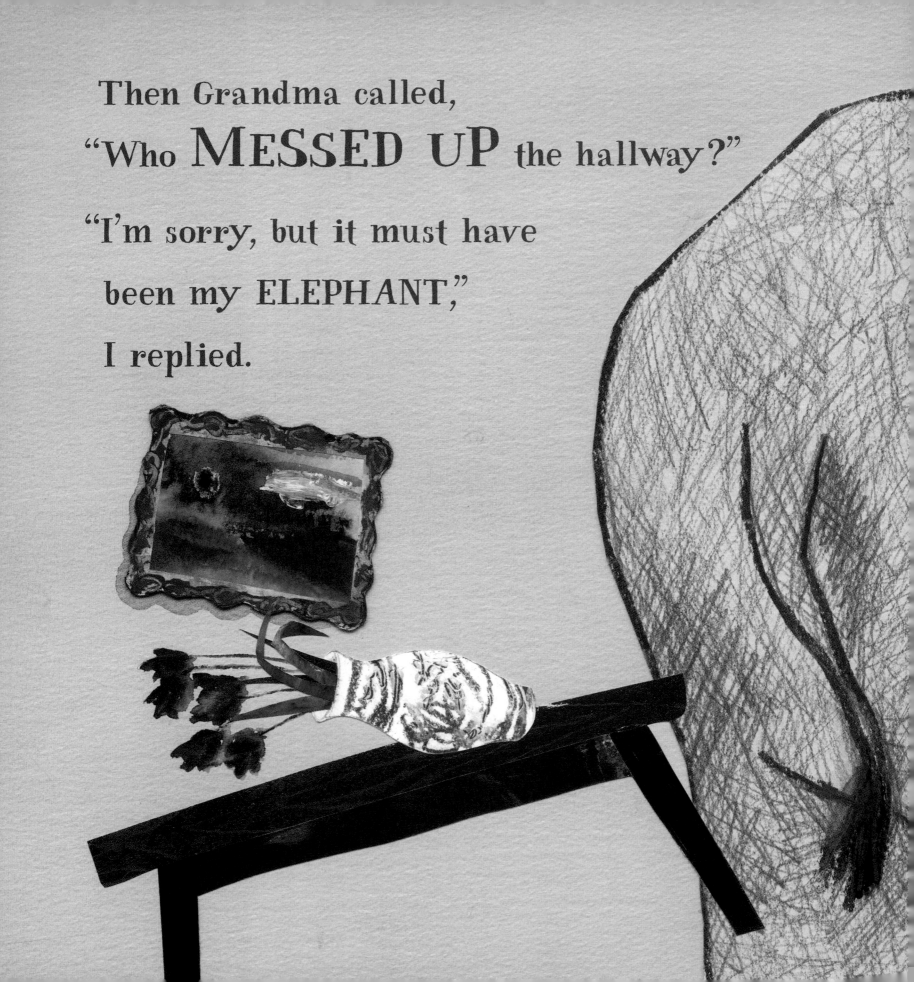

"And was it your
ELEPHANT
who

SPLASHED

and

made

puddles

in the

bathroom?"

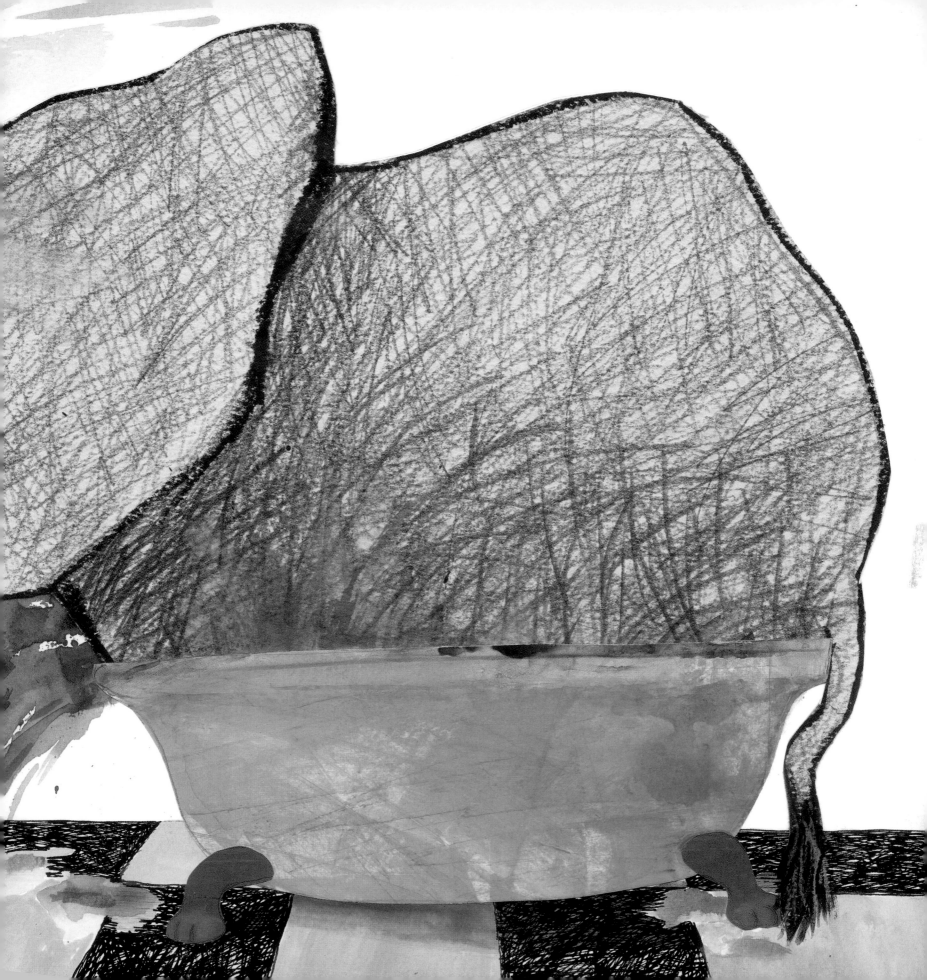

"And was it your ELEPHANT who ATE some of the cakes?" Grandma asked.

"Well ... yes," I replied truthfully. Grandma looked at me as if she didn't believe me.

I was upset.

I wanted
to be
alone.

Then my ELEPHANT came. He smiled at me. I said sorry for telling on him.

We were friends again.

We played in my room all day.

We went fishing. It was fun.

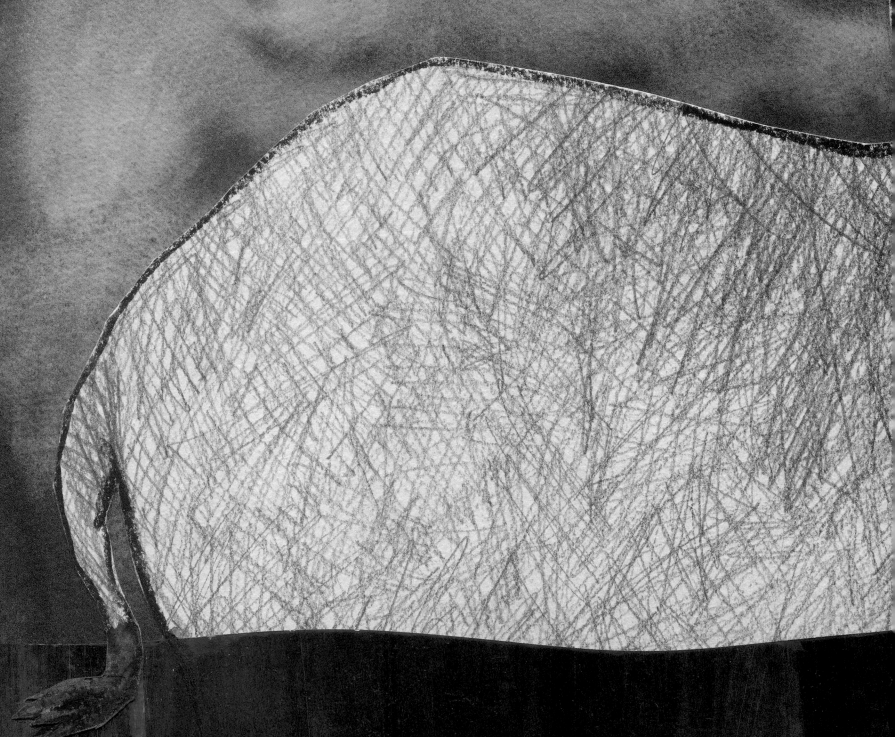

Then my ELEPHANT took me to
the jungle to see tigers until ...

it was
morning
and
Grandad
wanted
to play
football.

"But how did I get to bed?" I asked.

"You were tired..."

said Grandad.

"So your ELEPHANT took you to bed!"

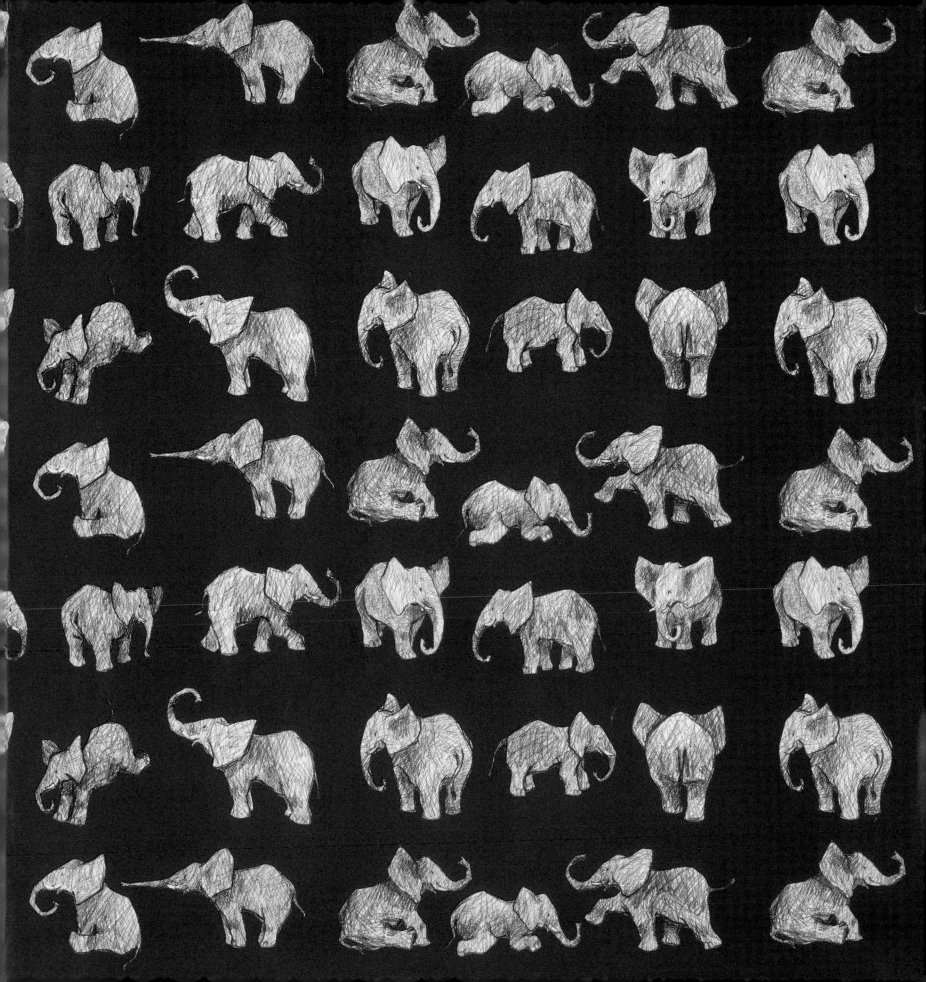

Other books by Petr Horáček

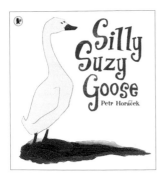

Silly Suzy Goose
ISBN 978-1-4063-0458-9

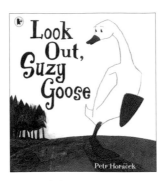

Look Out, Suzy Goose
ISBN 978-1-4063-1764-0

Suzy Goose and the Christmas Star
ISBN 978-1-4063-2621-5

Puffin Peter
ISBN 978-1-4063-3776-1

Night Night
ISBN 978-1-4063-2966-7

Creepy Crawly
ISBN 978-1-4063-2967-4

Choo Choo
ISBN 978-1-4063-2506-5

Beep Beep
ISBN 978-1-4063-2505-8

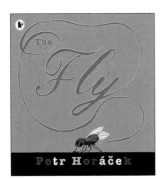

The Fly
ISBN 978-1-4063-3073-1

Butterfly Butterfly
ISBN 978-1-84428-844-1

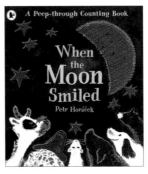

When the Moon Smiled
ISBN 978-0-7445-7047-2

A New House for Mouse
ISBN 978-1-4063-0122-9

This Little Cat
ISBN 978-1-4063-2511-9

Hello, Little Bird
ISBN 978-1-4063-2508-9

Run, Mouse, Run!
ISBN 978-1-4063-2509-6

Flutter By, Butterfly
ISBN 978-1-4063-2507-2

Strawberries are Red
ISBN 978-1-4063-2510-2

What is Black and White?
ISBN 978-1-4063-2512-6

Available from all good bookstores

www.walker.co.uk